A Best Friend's Betrayal & Revenge

Karma Comes For Hers

by Sheila Dorsey

Email: sdorsey1969@aol.com

Cover Design: I A.M. Editing, Ink

Interior Re-editor: Margaret Diehl

ISBN: 978-0-578-61588-2

Dedication

This book is dedicated to God for giving me the ability to write, and in the process, heal. This book is also dedicated to my beautiful family and best friend for always challenging me to strive for higher and better. Finally, this book is dedicated to all of the supporters who have purchased my very first book, *A Broken Child Saved by God's Grace*. Your positive feedback on how my writing has touched and/or ministered to you in some way means more than you know. I pray that this book may also persuade those who have caused or are still causing hurt upon others to change, forgive one another, and heal. To God, be the glory!

Table of Contents

Preface

This book was written because of the many supporters who encouraged me to continue writing. It is because of their anticipation of another book that I continued to write. Their kind and sincere words gave me the extra push that I needed to complete this project. To have people tell me that writing is my calling made me take a more in-depth look into developing myself as an author. Although my books are fiction, there is a lot of truth in them. I am positive this is why people have, can and will continue to relate to them. It is my hope that those who read my book will learn the importance of forgiveness and extend it toward others. For those of you that wanted more from me, here you are.

Introduction

Tina Robinson and Rhonda Berry were best friends as far back as they could remember. They were born and raised in Phoenix, Arizona, and lived diagonally across the street from each other. Rhonda was the sister Tina never had. They were so close and practically shared everything. They shared clothes (except undergarments), shoes, homework, driver licenses (they swapped them when they needed to), dreams, secrets, loyalty, ideas, trust, birthdays, etc. However, there was one thing that they could never share, and that was their love interests. There was a girl code in place that didn't allow it. The girl code was never spoken of, but its presence was known around the world. Unfortunately, Tina's curiosity drove her to break the universal girl code, which led Tina and Rhonda into a tailspin of powerful emotions and unthinkable acts. Little did they know, karma was coming for them both, and she didn't even think twice.

"Dearly beloved, avenge not yourselves, but rather give place unto wrath: for it is written, Vengeance is mine; I will repay, saith the Lord" (King James Version, Rom. 12.19).

Chapter 1
The Betrayal

Tina met Wendell Raynor, a football jock, one evening at Rhonda's house while they were hanging out after Leonard High School's football game. She knew of him but had never met him. He stood about six feet tall and had a chiseled athletic physique. He had short blond hair with ocean blue eyes. He was Thomas Beaudoin and David Beckham all rolled into one. He was total eye candy, and all the girls wanted him. However, he did not want all the girls. He only had eyes for Tina's best friend, Rhonda. It was discovered early on that Wendell loved himself some chocolate. He was a lover of dark chocolate, to be exact!

Rhonda met Wendell through her youngest brother, Webster Berry. Wendell and Webster were best friends, so he was always at Webster's house. Wendell's mom wasn't too fond of other races, which is why they never really hung out at his house. Rhonda and Wendell had a strong liking for each other but were not in a relationship. Rhonda was taking her time getting to know him. Being attracted to a white guy was completely out of her comfort zone. She had never had sex with a white person. Even though Wendell belonged to Rhonda, so to speak, and was strictly off-limits, Tina couldn't help but notice that he was extraordinarily handsome and fine for a white guy.

Tina was a single teenaged mom of a beautiful daughter, with no expectations. Tina and Webster were in the same boat as Rhonda and Wendell, meaning they were not in a relationship. They just cared a great deal for each other. It was known that Webster was still a virgin, and that made things a tad awkward for Tina. They had not once shared a hug or kiss. He was a church boy and was very cautious about who his first time would be with. He was in no hurry to lose his virginity and did not adhere to the pressure of his peers. All four of them got along well and were always together.

One Friday night after the game, Wendell suggested that they all go to Pizza Hut for dinner, and everyone agreed. He picked them up at Rhonda's house in his orange and black 1970 Dodge Challenger, and they left from there. Before that night, Tina noticed that Wendell would catch her gaze and stare longer than what would be considered normal as if he was trying to say something to her with his eyes. Each time, she turned away without giving any extra thought to those bizarre moments. Neither Rhonda nor Webster ever noticed.

Rhonda sat in the front passenger seat, and Tina and Webster jumped in the back seat, Tina behind the driver's seat and Webster behind his sister. Suddenly, Tina felt something rub across her left lower leg. She was about to scream because she thought something was crawling on her but quickly suppressed the urge when she realized it was Wendell's strong manly left hand reaching back down between the driver's seat and door. She looked up into the rear-view mirror and found him staring intensely into her beautiful brown eyes. She knew she should have nipped this in the bud at that very moment by telling Rhonda and Webster what Wendell was doing, but she was now fascinated with his pursuit. This man was driving the car with his right hand and touching her with his left hand, which turned Tina on in a twisted sort of way. This carried on for the entire duration of the twenty-minute ride. No one suspected a thing.

Once they got to the restaurant, they all sat down at a table, one love interest across from the other. The table had the Pac-Man game built into it so that you could look down at the game through the tabletop. The controllers to operate the game were located on each side along with money slots to pay for the game. Somehow, Wendell was able to pull off playing footsie with Tina under the table. At this point, she was trying to figure out his motive. What did he want from her? Did he think that because she already had a kid, she was an easy lay? Was he frustrated with Rhonda because she was moving to slow for his taste? Why did he suddenly have a strong desire to pursue her? She would need the answers to these questions soon because now she was very confused. They all finished dinner, and Wendell dropped them back off at Rhonda's. Then Tina walked home.

Tina could hardly wait for that following Friday so that she could see if it was just a one-time thing. Sure enough, it was the same routine, except they were all going to a Denny's. Only this time during the car ride when Wendell began to rub her leg, she grabbed onto the back of the driver's seat with both hands pretending to look for something on the floor. This was her opportunity to return a gentle rub on his arm – her way of letting him know that she was down for whatever. Tina knew that she was in big trouble with this guy. She needed to know his story, and it was evident that he wanted to know hers. Again, Wendell dropped everyone off at Rhonda's house after dinner.

Another Friday night after a football game, Tina ran into Wendell on his way to the locker room to shower. He whispered in her ear to meet him in front of classroom A103 in about twenty minutes. It was dark near that classroom. He chose that place because the entryway to the door had a ten-foot indentation. He knew Tina wouldn't be caught. Just like Wendell requested, Tina was standing right outside the classroom door of A103.

When Wendell arrived, they hugged each other tightly as if they had been apart for years. Then they kissed each other so intensely that they both ended up leaning onto the classroom door. They felt the fireworks inside and knew there was something to this chemistry that they shared. His deep sexy voice resonated throughout her entire body. Tina and Wendell wanted to explore these feelings more, which meant that they would need to spend time together. This also meant that they would need to become more creative on how they were going to sneak around to be with each other.

After they came up for air from that kiss, they talked, laughed, and got to know each other a little more. Tina was finally able to get all of her questions answered. It turned out that Wendell thought she was a beautiful young lady whom he really wanted to get to know. He didn't have a sinister motive. Tina believed him but also felt that he was intrigued and wanted to see what it would be like to be with someone of a different race.

While they were talking, Tina found out that Rhonda and Wendell were about to have sex one day at Rhonda's house a long while ago before he chased after Tina. Someone came home early and interrupted them, so they didn't get a chance to. Tina was happy to hear that. Her poor heart would have been devastated. They then separated, walking in opposite directions, to meet up with Rhonda and Webster so that it wouldn't appear that they were together.

After they left, they had dinner at Rhonda's house and played board games. It was almost unbearable for Tina and Wendell to sit there and pretend like nothing was going on between them when all they wanted to do was be together, alone. They kept their composure because they knew that they would get to see each other next week and be alone, enjoying each other's company without having to hide. They had already hatched an elaborate plan.

That next Saturday came, and their plan was underway. Tina had told Rhonda that she was hanging out with Tammy Quaker, one of her school friends, and Wendell told Webster that he was hanging out with his brother most of the day. Tina's best friend, Raven Sparks, would babysit her daughter when she met with Wendell.

Tina walked to the playground over in the next neighborhood, which is where Wendell picked her up from in his sports car, and they drove to his mom's house. He never talked about his dad, so Tina assumed he wasn't in his life and didn't ask any questions.

This day Tina and Wendell were going to take things to the next level. They were going to make love in his bedroom, or so they thought. They were in the room getting cozy when Wendell's brother knocked frantically on the door to let Wendell know that their mom came home for lunch. Wendell's brother was in the family room watching TV when their mom drove into the driveway. Wendell instructed Tina to hide in his closet because his mom was not very fond of black people. She did it because she didn't want him to get in any trouble, and she didn't want to get caught.

An hour later, his mom went back to work, and Tina came out of the closet. She told Wendell to take her back to the playground so that she could walk back home. It was obvious that she was angry that he didn't tell his mom about her, and she gave him a piece of her mind on the ride back. She wasn't so angry that she couldn't give him a goodbye kiss, though. Their plans were blown for that day, but they would soon have a chance to make up for it. They planned to meet the following Saturday at the same playground.

Next Saturday came, and nothing was going to ruin this day for them. They met as they had planned right at dusk to avoid being seen. Wendell parked his sports car in one of the intimate spots outside of the park near the lake. They sat there listening to music, talking, laughing, hugging, and kissing for about an hour.

Wendell asked Tina, "Do you want to get into the back seat?"

Tina replied, "Yes!"

He first climbed between the driver and passenger seats to the back seat, and Tina followed suit. She straddled his lap as they continued to hug and kiss. Looking into each other eyes said they wanted more, right then and there. Tina was a little hesitant to go further with Wendell because this would be the second white guy she'd ever been with sexually. She had heard rumors that white guys were not big in the genital area, and the first white guy she encountered proved that to be true. So, she was sure this would be the case with him.

Wendell unbuckled his belt, unbuttoned and unzipped his jeans, and pulled them along with his boxers down to his ankles. Tina saw quickly that he was well endowed and that the rumors were just myths. Tina had on a knee-high skirt. She raised her body in the air enough to pull her panties completely off and placed them into her purse.

They begin to hug and kiss again, both very excited. Wendell then grabbed her brown leather saddle (her hips and all that's between) with both hands and mounted it on top of his Cremello (white/cream-colored horse). They then began to gallop furiously toward the finish line as if they were both trying to win the first-place ribbons and trophies at the horse show.

It's a good thing they were in a hidden area because between the loud whinnying, the calling of Wendell's name, the rocking of the car, and the foggy windows, someone would have called the police on them for disturbing the peace. Once they crossed that finish line, they shared a celebratory embrace and long steamy kiss. That Cremello stallion hit the right spot, and oh what a ride it was. One she would never forget.

They didn't want to part ways but knew they had to go home before it got too late. He loved the way it felt to be inside of her, and she loved the way he felt inside of her. Wendell pulled his boxers and jeans back up and fixed his belt. Tina pulled her panties out of her purse and put them back on. It was at that moment that Wendell told Tina that she was the first African-American girl he'd been with sexually and that he was in love with her. She expressed that she was in love with him, as well. He insisted on driving Tina home this time, but they still had to be careful and stay on the down-low. Rhonda and Webster could not find out.

There were several entryways into Tina's neighborhood. Wendell took the entryway into the neighborhood where he would have to drive past Rhonda and Webster's house. He blew the horn and waved as he drove by, indicating that he couldn't stop. He'd done this before, so this was not out of the ordinary. Tina was in the passenger seat but had reclined the seat all the way back so that no one could see her. Wendell drove her around the block and stopped at a corner within walking distance of her house. He kissed her goodbye and drove off in the same direction from which he came. This time on his way back through the neighborhood, he stopped to visit Rhonda and Webster. Tina waited about twenty minutes before she walked to her house so as not to raise any suspicion. Soon, sneaking around became their norm.

At this point in their relationship, Tina and Wendell were in each other's nostrils and had entered each other's bloodstream. They were each other's oxygen and needed each other to breathe. They couldn't wait to feel each other again, and they didn't have to wait much longer.

One Wednesday during school, they decided to skip fourth-period class and meet each other at Wendell's car in the student parking lot. Once in the car, they quickly got undressed from the waist down and spent the entire class period making love in the back seat of his car. Only this time, he positioned Tina up against the door in a way that allowed him to have full control of entering her body.

She had nowhere to run and had no choice but to envelop all of him with each mesmerizing stroke. He gave her pain and pleasure, and she enjoyed them both. He was determined to make their bodies become one that day.

Wendell took his sweet, gentle time with Tina. He "slow rhythm and blues-ed" her until she hit that high octave note while singing his name in their chorus of what they thought was love. He then followed with his own drum pounding at a fast rate, sending him into a soulful melody that Tina could not get enough of. She loved his sexy deep voice, especially when he called her name.

Oddly enough, they had never performed oral transactions on each other. Time was running out, so they swiftly got dressed, kissed, and headed back into the school's courtyard just in time to hear the bell for their next class period.

Tina and Wendell knew that they would see each other again real soon at the Phoenix Community Center on Saturday evening. They also knew that all four of them, including Rhonda and Webster, would be together. They figured that the two of them would surely have an opportunity to sneak away for a moment.

Saturday evening arrived, and the high school soirée had just begun at the Phoenix Community Center. The center was jam-packed with students, family, and friends. There was dancing, drinking (wine and liquor), and smoking (weed). You name it, and it was going on at this party. Although alcohol and drugs were not allowed, they somehow made their way inside the building.

The four amigos had arrived and were all

ready to have a good time. Tina and Wendell were just waiting for the chance to be able to sneak away and meet outside at the back of the building. Because it was so crowded and everyone was mingling, they decided that now would be the perfect time to make their way to the spot. They were so happy to see each other and be alone that they held each other tightly as they passionately kissed. It was like their lives depended on it.

There was no one outside but them, which meant their plan worked. No one noticed that they had disappeared from inside the building. They planned to continue this love affair forever and were certain that no one would ever find out.

Tina and Wendell had really done it now! Didn't they realize that they were betraying the only true best friends they had for moments of lust they had mistaken for love? They were only concerned about their own selfish needs, which was to feed their flesh when it was hungry. Their love-lust story was about to end abruptly. Tina, Webster, Rhonda, and Wendell's worlds were about to be rocked to the core.

A Real Friend

I, a real friend, made a mistake and crossed the line.

I, a real friend, messed around with a guy who wasn't mine.

I, a real friend, knew better from the start.

I, a real friend, helped harden your heart.

I, a real friend, know I lost your trust.

I, a real friend, went after love that really was lust.

I, a real friend, took things too far.

I, a real friend, left you with that scar.

I, a real friend, claimed to be the realest.

I, a real friend, wanted forgiveness.

I, a real friend, was lost, it seemed.

I, a real friend, by God, was redeemed.

Chapter 2
They Found Out

S till engaged in French kissing their butts off, Tina and Wendell didn't even realize the back door of the Phoenix Community Center had been opened until it was too late. Once they heard the door slam closed, they quickly let go of each other and turned toward the sound. To their surprise, Webster was standing there just looking at them. They were all staring at each other, wondering what each other was going to do or say.

Once it sunk in that Webster had just seen the girl he really liked and his best friend making out as if this wasn't their first time, an array of emotions came over him. His facial expressions displayed shock, disappointment, anger, and then disgust. Tina could tell that she had deeply hurt Webster. She was aware that he was really into her, but she couldn't help that she was in love with Wendell. She apologized to Webster and walked back into the building. Wendell placed both hands on his head and paced back and forth, saying, "Webster, man, I'm sorry!" They then went their separate ways.

Tina, still reeling from what had just happened and riddled with guilt, found friends with bottles of wine. She took one and drank it all by herself until she was drunk. She knew it would only be a matter of time before Webster told his sister, Rhonda, that he caught her and Wendell in action. She just couldn't deal. She knew that their behavior was reprehensible. Now she was faced with losing Webster, her best friend, and her man.

Tina was ready to go home from the party, but her ride was not ready to leave just yet. So, she walked in the direction of her house until a few friends from her neighborhood offered her a ride home, which she gladly accepted.

Webster decided to wait until he got home from the party to tell Rhonda what he saw. After they arrived, Webster followed Rhonda into her room and closed the door. He didn't want their parents to hear what was going on. Webster told her that he saw Tina and Wendell sucking face behind the building at the party that night. He went on to tell her that this did not appear to be their first-time tongue wrestling. He believed that they had been messing around for a while based on the way they were holding each other.

Webster and Rhonda were both angry, as they had a right to be. When Webster left to go to bed, Rhonda sat on the edge of her bed and cursed out Tina and Wendell in her mind. *How dare they betray our friendship, loyalty, and trust! Who do they think they are?* She then began to pack everything that Tina left at her house in a brown paper bag, including anything that she had given her as a gift. She wanted to let Tina know just how angry she was and that she meant serious business.

The next day, Rhonda, still mad about what had transpired the previous night, headed to Tina's house with the paper bag full of items. She marched over as if she was going to battle. She knocked on Tina's front door and waited for an answer. Rhonda wasn't sure who was going to answer the door, but she didn't care who did. The door opened and revealed Tina standing there.

"Webster told me what happened. Is it true?"

Tina looking down at the ground and replied, "Yes, and I'm so sorry!"

The guilt she carried wouldn't allow her to look directly into Rhonda's eyes. Rhonda, with a cantankerous demeanor, threw the brown paper bag in Tina's face so hard that it knocked her back a little. She told Tina to never speak to her again and that they were no longer friends.

Rhonda stormed off back to her house and did not once look back. Tina's first reaction (prepared to fight) was to pick up the paper bag off the porch and throw it at the back of Rhonda's head, but she didn't because she felt that she had already done enough. Instead, Tina picked up the paper bag off the porch and yelled, "I'm sorry, Rhonda. Please forgive me!" Rhonda acted as though she didn't even hear her, forcing her to retreat to her room in pain and tears. Their friendship was never supposed to end and not in this way. After all, this was her best friend. She began to wonder if falling in love with Wendell was even worth all of this. Rhonda couldn't even stand to look at Tina. She knew that she could never see Wendell again after that.

A few days later, Wendell mustered up enough nerve to go over to his best friend's house to talk to him. He wanted things to go back to the way they were. He was very nervous, and his heart was beating faster with each step he took. He wasn't sure if Webster was going to swing on him or not. He really didn't want to have to fight his best friend. He had never seen him that angry before.

Wendell knocked on the door, and Webster

stepped outside to listen to what he had to say. Wendell noticed that Webster was in a much better mood than the night of the party and felt that now would be a perfect time to apologize again, face to face.

"I don't know what came over me, but I made a mistake and fell in love with Tina. I didn't mean to, but it just happened." Wendell apologized to Webster about ten times before they shook hands and hugged each other. Wendell knew that he couldn't be caught anywhere near Tina after getting things back on track.

Wendell was now hanging out again at Webster and Rhonda's house, which meant that he would most definitely have to be in her presence. When Rhonda saw Wendell, she slapped him so hard that she left her handprint across his face. His face turned completely red. He wasn't really in shock because he knew that he deserved what he had gotten. He played with her feelings, and she wasn't having it. He apologized to her for what he had done, but Rhonda wasn't listening to anything he said.

After that day, Wendell came over to Webster and Rhonda's house several times, and she wouldn't even speak to him. She would roll her eyes and pretend that he wasn't there. At that point, she couldn't stand the ground that he walked upon.

Webster saw Tina walking past his house one day and called her name. She looked in his direction as he began to walk toward her. They met up at the end of his driveway. Before he could utter a word, Tina said that she was sorry for everything that she caused. Webster accepted her apology, but not before he made her feel his wrath.

"I cared a lot for you. I was going to ask you to be my girlfriend eventually. I was willing to accept you even though you already have a child, and this is how you repay me? By sleeping with my best friend?" He continued, "I'm glad that I didn't lose my virginity to you." Tina hung her head in shame. As she began to walk away, Webster said, "Hey, I forgive you because I don't hold grudges." Tina slightly smiled and kept walking. She only wished Rhonda would soon accept her apology as well.

Tina never got to say goodbye to Wendell. They didn't have a chance at a proper closure. She heard through the grapevine that he had joined the United States Marine Corps and already left town for basic training. She didn't get to look in his eyes. She didn't get to hug him. She didn't get to kiss or make love to him one last time. She wondered if he was thinking about her and missing her like she was him.

Everything was out in the open now. Tina was without a best friend, a potential boyfriend, and her man all because they found out.

Chapter 3
The Plot Thickens

After about two weeks, Rhonda finally accepted Tina's apology and started talking to her again. They began to hang out like before as if nothing had happened. Although they were damaged individuals and had gone through many vicissitudes in life, Tina loved having her best friend back. She had vowed to Rhonda that she would never do anything like that again within their friendship. In fact, whenever Tina liked or wanted to date someone, she would ask Rhonda if she had ever slept with the guy. If the answer was yes, Tina would keep it moving. Rhonda would do the same for the most part. They were inseparable.

Rhonda met a very handsome man one day on her way to the corner store. His name was Hyatt Future. He asked for her home phone number, and she gave it to him. They began talking and eventually dating. Soon they were officially boyfriend and girlfriend. Hyatt was ten years her senior. Rhonda didn't tell Tina much about Hyatt, especially about their lovemaking behavior. Perhaps, she was afraid that Tina would want to try him out for herself like she had done Wendell.

They appeared to be madly in love with one another. Within that love, they conceived a beautiful baby boy. Nothing or no one could interrupt Rhonda and Hyatt's love. Well, no one except Rhonda and her thirst for revenge upon Tina. It was almost like she was a wild beast in the jungle searching for her next prey. She was pleased with her relationship, and the next step in her life should have been marriage. So, why was she still on this quest to shake up Tina's world? Rhonda was desperately out to settle the score. Tina had met this cutie by the name of Hakeem Williams, who was extremely fine. Some said he looked like Michael Jackson but with a Ginuwine body.

They didn't waste any time hooking up and getting into a full-fledged relationship one night after going to a teen club. They knew each other from the neighborhood. Tina began to constantly talk about Hakeem, especially when she was around Rhonda. Of course, she spoke about him because she was in love with him. She glowed at Hakeem. She had a smile on her face as wide as Phoenix, AZ, from being so happy.

Rhonda, in the background, was observing this all unfolding. She was just waiting for the perfect time to make her move. She waited until Tina had fallen deep for Hakeem. She figured what she was about to do would hurt Tina, which is what she wanted. She wanted the pain she was about to cause to sting and knock Tina off her game. Rhonda began to set her trap for Tina and Hakeem.

On the school bus ride from school one day, Tina's friend Tammy saw Rhonda sitting on Hakeem's lap outside of an apartment. The two sat in a chair for the whole world to see. Tammy knew this had to be a joke. Or else Hakeem had lost his mind to do such a thing, especially in public. In fact, this was all a part of Rhonda's plan, the start of her seduction. Tammy couldn't wait to tell Tina what she saw. She ran home and called Tina.

"Are you and Hakeem still together?"

"Of course! That's my man, and I love him! Why in the world did you ask me that?"

"Well, I just saw Rhonda sitting in his lap like they were a couple in front of an apartment on my way home from school today."

Why on earth would Rhonda be sitting on Hakeem's lap? That meant that she was all up in his personal space. She was a little angry and jealous, and then she blurted out to Tammy, "My man would never cheat on me! He knows he's got a good thing and doesn't need another girl."

He told her on several occasions, usually after sex, that he would never cheat on her because she was the best that he'd ever had. She had a sense of confidence and cockiness when she said it. Tammy knew what she had seen, and it looked like some cheating was going on to her.

She didn't say anything else to Tina about it because she could see that Tina was convinced that nothing was going on with Rhonda and Hakeem. It had to be just a friendly game of musical chairs, and Rhonda just happened to land on his lap. Not to mention, they were the only two playing this game, outside, in public, with no music.

When Tina finished her phone call with Tammy, she still had the thought of her man and Rhonda together in the back of her mind. She was waiting for the right opportunity to bring it up to Hakeem so that he could quickly clear up this mishap. By the time that Tina realized what Rhonda was doing, it was too late.

Rhonda had already left a trail of dangerous venom. A few days prior, she had asked Tina to

21

babysit her son while she and Hyatt went out on a date. Tina didn't hesitate to say yes. After all, she was a sucker for love. She and her best friend were in relationships and in love.

When Friday came, Tina was babysitting Rhonda's son as planned, and two hours later, Rhonda and Hyatt knocked on the door. When Tina opened the door, she could tell they had been arguing about something.

As soon as they walked inside, Hyatt said to Tina, "I don't know why you are sitting here babysitting for Rhonda while she's out sleeping with your man!"

Tina was in total shock. Rhonda stood silent, holding her son on her hip. She didn't deny what her boyfriend just said. Instead, she walked out the door and left. No eye contact, no I didn't sleep with your boyfriend, no nothing!

Tina was still confused. So, Hyatt cleared up the confusion for her. He let Tina know that Rhonda was not out on a date with him but with Hakeem instead. Apparently, they had made plans to meet up to have sex to get back at Tina. Rhonda had explained to Hakeem what Tina did to her in the past and that she wanted to get even. Hakeem was down for it, and Rhonda's seduction didn't help.

"How do you know all of this?" Tina asked Hyatt.

"Your boyfriend got drunk after he screwed my girl and started running his mouth."

Hakeem was bragging about having had sex with his girl's best friend in the backseat of his car, just like Tina had done with Wendell. That news quickly got back to Hyatt as he waited for Rhonda in front of Tina's house to pick up their son. Eventually,

22

when everything slowed down, and Rhonda and Hyatt cooled off, they decided to work their relationship issues out. On the other hand, Tina and Hakeem had yet to talk.

The very next day, Tina was at Hakeem's house at the crack of dawn, waiting to confront him about cheating on her with Rhonda. He came onto the lanai where Tina was standing and reached out to give her a hug and kiss as usual. Tina aggressively pushed him away in disgust as if he had a contagious disease.

"Did you give what belongs to me, to Rhonda?" He attempted to change the subject by stating how much he loved her and how he would never intentionally hurt her. He also noted that Rhonda meant nothing to him. He was drunk, and anything could have happened.

Obviously, he thought Tina was a fool who couldn't read between the lines. He had just indirectly admitted to her that he had intercourse with Rhonda. Tina was afraid to ask him if they had oral sex as well because she genuinely didn't want to know the answer to that. She probably would have tried to murder him on the spot. After more arguing and crying, Tina forgave him. They really loved each other. Tina and Hakeem, just like Rhonda and Hyatt, decided to work their problems out and stay together, which only lasted a little while longer.

Tina was not able to trust Hakeem or Rhonda after that. Her heart was crushed. Tina believed this was what it must have felt like when Rhonda found out that she and Wendell were messing around back then. The only difference was, Rhonda and Wendell were not in a relationship, nor were they in love with each other.

To her mind, the offenses were not the same.

Tina's thoughts had a pernicious influence on what she physically wanted to do to Rhonda. She couldn't believe that this girl sat around for almost two years, pretending to have genuinely accepted her apology and had forgiven her while still carrying vengeance in her heart. She had planned this whole scenario.

Who does that? Rhonda delighted in what she had done to Tina, but she wasn't ready for what happened next.

Two Wrongs

It's said that two wrongs don't make a right, but what about for the person that's been wronged?

Two wrongs can wreak havoc on people's hearts and minds.

Two wrongs can make certain situations seem justifiable.

Two wrongs make for behemoth egos.

Two wrongs do not discriminate.

No matter how the story goes, two wrongs are never right.

Chapter 4
The Revenge

Hyatt, still not happy with the fact that Rhonda cheated on him with Tina's boyfriend, wanted to get a little revenge of his own. He consistently pursued Tina, reminding her of how Rhonda made them both look like fools. It went in one of Tina's ears and out of the other. She really meant to never stoop to that level again and betray Rhonda in any way. So, Tina turned Hyatt down every time he propositioned her. She knew that he really loved Rhonda and was hurting inside, knowing that he had given this girl everything that she asked for, including his seed. He practically treated her like a queen, and she risked throwing it all away just to get back at Tina.

Tina was determined to remain best friends with Rhonda because she truly valued their friendship. She could only trust her as far as she could see her, though. It was odd that Tina could trust Rhonda with all other aspects of her life, like with money and her child, but could not trust her around her man. Rhonda probably felt the same way about her.

As time went on, when Rhonda and Tina would hang out, Rhonda had the unmitigated gall to take jabs at Tina by bringing up things about when she and Hakeem had sex. Tina would ignore her or change the subject, but Rhonda kept on taking digs at her with comments that suggested that Hakeem may have enjoyed her in the sack more than Tina. Tina became enraged but did not let Rhonda know that she was. In the back of her mind, she knew that Hyatt was going to step to her again, begging for her sweet nectar. Although she turned him down at first, Rhonda's behavior changed her mind.

Sure enough, Hyatt ran into Tina again and offered her the world just to be with him for one night. He was a drug dealer who also had a legit full-time job so that the police wouldn't have any indication of what he was doing. This time, she accepted his sexual advances. However, she wasn't fazed by the material things that he could offer her. They talked and made plans to meet up on that upcoming Friday night. They even decided that they were going to keep the incident to themselves. They just wanted to have something to hold over Rhonda and Hakeem's head. It would be their little secret.

Hyatt picked Tina up that Friday night down the road from her house and drove to his sister's house, which he shared with her. Once they arrived, he escorted Tina into the house. She was wearing a tricolored maxi sundress with matching sandals. He was wearing a pair of jeans and a casual polo shirt with matching sneakers.

He was quite the gentleman. He waited on her hand and foot. He served her dinner, engaged her in great conversation. They slow danced a little to some smooth jazz. He danced her over to the pool table in the entertainment room. They did not once kiss each other. It wasn't that kind of arrangement. They knew what they were there for, and it was time to get to it.

Hyatt slowly began to put hickeys on Tina's neck so that he could leave reminders, which would possibly make Rhonda wonder where Tina got those passion kisses from. Hyatt gently laid Tina across the pool table, lifted her sundress, and pulled her panties to the side. He was yearning to taste her flavor. This was not a part of the deal, but she didn't stop him. She just knew that she was not returning the favor.

Before he placed his face between her thighs, he whispered in her ear, saying, "You remind me of the limited-edition chocolate Twinkies with extra cream in the middle." He had to have a great deal of tenacity to make so many juices come down her delicate pocket. Tina was dripping so much that she didn't even notice that he had dropped his pants and slid his pool stick inside of her. After five full strokes, he had already finished his game of pool. He hit the eight ball into the pocket before the game really got started. Tina was okay with that, for he had already let her win the first game with the white ball.

After fixing his clothes, Hyatt helped Tina off the pool table back onto her feet. They exited the house the way they came, and he proceeded to drive her back to the spot where he had picked her up. They said goodbye and knew that was the first and last time they would get down like that.

The next day Tina went over to Rhonda's house, intending to let her see the hickeys on her neck without letting her know what went down the night before. Rhonda asked Tina, "Who put those love bites on your neck?"

Before Tina knew it, she replied quickly, "Hyatt did!" Rhonda rolled her eyes at her and walked into the kitchen.

Tina was watching her every move because she wanted to see her reaction. Rhonda's mom had cooked homemade banana pudding, which Tina saw on the kitchen counter.

"Fix me a bowl of banana pudding!" Rhonda did as she was aggressively instructed to do. Tina was being mean and downright rude to her. Rhonda appeared to be somewhat scared, and Tina was enjoying it. The way Tina felt, if Rhonda had said anything wrong, they probably would have fought right there in the middle of the kitchen. Somehow, they still managed to hold on to the shred of friendship they had left.

Tina thought that boning Hyatt and bullying Rhonda would make her feel better, but it made her feel worse. She felt as small as a grain of dirt. She was disappointed in herself because she had broken the vow that she had made to Rhonda. Although she did not come straight out and tell Rhonda that she and Hyatt were together sexually, she implied it. Tina never brought up anything about her and Hyatt ever again. She was back to sticking with the vow that she had made regardless of what Rhonda would or would not do next. Rhonda and Hyatt's relationship didn't last much longer after that because he found out that she was cheating on him with another guy. That guy turned out to be the real father of her son. Talk about surprised!

Tina wanted to tell Hakeem what she had done with Hyatt, but she decided not to. He had no clue about how down and dirty they had gotten. Hyatt wasn't the type of man that would get drunk and brag about his business as Hakeem had previously done. There were times, though, that Tina wondered if Rhonda had been with Hakeem more than once but didn't dare question him to find out. She was done with the going back and forth. Hakeem and Tina's relationship dwindled because he had cheated on her with a much older woman who stole his heart. It took her a while to get over it and move on, but at least she still had her friendship with Rhonda or, so she thought. Just because Tina was done, didn't mean Rhonda was. Rhonda didn't make a vow, Tina did.

Chapter 5
Two Can Play That Game

Several years later while Tina was at basic training at Phoenix Love Police Academy (PLPA), she would call home on Sundays to talk to her mom and check on her family. During one of their phone conversations, Tina's mom interrupted her by saying, "Guess who I saw together at Walmart the other day?"

"Who?"

"Rhonda and Mr. Jerome Wright."

She couldn't believe what she'd heard. Did her mom really see her ex and Rhonda together as if they were a couple? Her mom said that they had looked at her like deer caught in headlights. Like they were busted doing something that they shouldn't have been doing. This was a man that Tina once loved. Back in the day, they lived together for six months and were practically married (in her fantasy world). That was until she caught him on the phone with another woman, put him out, and bleached everything that he owned.

Tina had shared this information with Rhonda, so why was she now with her ex? Could she not find her own man? Tina wasn't sure why this news bothered her because she was in a relationship with someone new. After all, she and Jerome didn't work out because he chose the streets (drugs, alcohol, etc.) over her. Maybe it was the fact that she had to hear the news from her mom instead of her best friend, Rhonda. Tina would be graduating from basic training soon and on her way home.

Tina had been home for two weeks now and still no word from Rhonda. Any other time when she would go away for an extended period of time, she would see Rhonda on her first day back. Perhaps Rhonda was hiding from her. She had to know that Tina's mom had already told her that she and Jerome were together. Maybe she didn't know how to approach her. Tina found out soon enough that Jerome was living with Rhonda. That explained her awkward absence.

Tina decided to visit her one afternoon to see what she would say and how she would react in her presence. She knocked on the door, and Rhonda's son answered the door. Once she entered the apartment, she saw Rhonda and Jerome staring at her in shock.

Tina decided to break the ice by telling Rhonda to come over and give her a hug. She even hugged Jerome. Tina smiled and said to them both, "Y'all know y'all wrong for this, but I still love ya."

Tina and Rhonda talked for a little while longer, catching up on her police academy endeavors. Jerome went back into the bedroom, shaking his head with a smirk on his face because their impromptu meeting turned out better than he had expected. The fact that he and Rhonda were still alive after Tina arrived was proof of that.

Seeing Jerome again was nostalgic for Tina. She remembered all the great memories they once shared. The brother was still tall and fine. He still had big hands and big feet. She remembered that this man could go deep in every sense of the word. This made her want to know the real reason why he was with

Rhonda. She really wasn't his type.

Tina confronted Jerome when he was by himself at his uncle's house to inquire about how he and Rhonda became a couple. He informed her that she ran after him on five different occasions, and he told her and showed her that he was not interested. He was like, "You know I was in a serious relationship with Tina in the past." The last time she offered him her services, he finally gave in. She literally would flash him her snatch. To Tina, that should have been more of a reason for him to not have given in. It was just too easy to get. However, Jerome was caught at a very weak moment. He began to think that he and Tina would never get back together anyway, so why not hook up with Rhonda. She provided him with a place to stay, drugs to get high, food to eat, and sex. How could he walk away from that, especially when he was hopping from one relative's couch to another? That was his stability for the time being. They used each other for what they needed. He had to do what he had to do. Tina couldn't knock him for his hustle. It's called survival of the fittest! He would always say, "I'm surviving out here in these streets."

Rhonda and Jerome's tumultuous relationship ended not long after Tina's surprise visit. It was clear to Rhonda that he still had some feelings for Tina. She also began to feel insecure and started asking questions like, "Do you still love her? Do you want to be with her again?" He didn't want to lie to her, so he just avoided her questions. He then started feeling like he couldn't stay at Rhonda's apartment anymore because he felt like he was so in the wrong. He felt like he was cheating on Tina even though they were not together in a relationship. He wasn't sure why he was feeling this way, but he knew he had to get out of this situation. Jerome always had a great deal of respect and love for Tina. Rhonda may have temporarily had his body, but Tina still owned his heart.

Will They Ever Be?

He loves her.
She loves him.
He wants to see her.
She wants to see him.
He wants to be with her.
She wants to be with him.
Will they ever be?

He is fighting addictions.

She is fighting remaining celibate until marriage this go 'round.

Will they ever be, or are they just wasting precious time?

Chapter 6
Enough Is Enough

After the incident with Jerome, Rhonda thought that Tina was going to strike again. Tina was very serious about being done with the sleeping around game of trying to get even. It didn't make her feel good at all. She had no intention of having sex with anyone else that Rhonda was involved with. She had learned her lesson the hard way. She didn't like it when the shoe was on the other foot. Her and Rhonda's relationship was never the same after that ordeal with Tina and Wendell. If contextualized, Rhonda and Tina's friendship was a tainted friendship that tried to prevail.

Tina had believed that Rhonda felt bad about getting revenge on her until she saw first-hand how she reveled in getting even with other people who she felt wronged her. It was very disturbing to see. She had no remorse.

Tina listened to Rhonda brag about how she slept with her cousin's husband in their bathroom and then ate dinner with them later that night while he still had her honeycomb juices in his mouth. She slept with him because she had left her boyfriend at her apartment in the family room with her cousin while she went to the corner store. When she returned, she noticed that her cousin and boyfriend were sweating. She figured it was because they were knocking boots on her couch. She questioned them aggressively and received the answer that they were dancing to the Nintendo Wii Just Dance game that was on. Rhonda was not satisfied with their responses, and shortly after, began to lure her cousin's husband into her beehive. It was like she needed sex, and her sexual appetite had grown tremendously.

Her behavior reminded Tina of the lady (Nola Darling) in the Spike Lee movie, *She's Gotta Have It*. At this point, Tina felt sorry for Rhonda and thought that she could somehow help her see what she was doing to herself and others.

Rhonda would always say to Tina, "Don't have sex for free." Rhonda's self-worth came with a price tag. Tina thought that Rhonda was worth far more than what she was getting from these different men and wondered if Rhonda knew her self-worth. It took time and many mistakes for Tina to finally learn hers. She was willing to show Rhonda what she had learned, but Rhonda had her unique way of doing things and really didn't care to hear what Tina had to say.

Tina expressed to Rhonda one of her fantasies, which was to watch Rhonda have wild sex with someone. She didn't want to be a part of it; she wanted to watch from inside the closet. Rhonda made it happen for Tina one night during a time when Tina was on vacation from the Phoenix Love Police Department.

Rhonda recruited one of her guy friends, who supposedly was in a committed relationship with another woman. I say supposedly because he never hesitated to come to Rhonda's apartment to get busy. When the guy arrived, Tina was already sitting in the closet.

He knew she was in there because Rhonda set the scene up. They undressed and began kissing, touching, sucking, licking, talking dirty, and grinding on each other. Then they started to engage in aggressive lovemaking.

Tina became very aroused inside the closet. Fifteen minutes later, she came out of the closet, undressing as she walked toward them on the bed and eventually joined in. Rhonda and her guy friend asked, "What took you so long?" She didn't answer. She just became very hands-on with the activities taking place and in some cases, mouth-on. She was doing things that she'd never imagined doing. However, she didn't allow the guy to penetrate her because he was beyond what she could handle or was accustomed to at that time.

She watched Rhonda ride him as she caressed Rhonda's breasts from behind. After everyone reached their climax several times, they all got dressed and went their separate ways. That was a night that they all would remember because it was their first time involved in a threesome.

Rhonda wanted to be with Tina sexually. Tina calmly explained to Rhonda that she wasn't down with that. Tina said that her curiosity got the best of her, and she wanted to know what it felt like to receive oral sex from a female. She had heard that a woman could do it better than a man because a woman knows what a woman likes. However, in her eyes, it felt the same, so she would just stick to men. That way, she could have the rod too.

Rhonda was shocked but had no choice but to respect Tina's wishes. She assumed that because she took Tina to an earth-shattering orgasm and called out her name that that would be the start of them messing around. Tina wasn't having it, though. After that day, they never spoke again about a threesome or having sex with each other. Tina couldn't help but wonder if Rhonda (who was bisexual) was trying to make her life a living hell because she couldn't have her to herself.

Rhonda had entered what Tina considered the married- man phase of life. She was messing around with a married man and literally thought that he was going to leave his wife for her. She fell in love with this man. Sure, he gave her money here and there, but she deserved so much more than what he was offering. She was worth far more than money could ever buy. She had very little of his time, and she obviously didn't have his heart. Otherwise, he wouldn't have left every time they had sex to go back home to his wife.

"You know that this is wrong, and he's not going to leave his wife," Tina told Rhonda.

"You messed with married men before, so how can you talk?"

"Yes, I did, but I stopped. I was convicted and learned my lesson. I apologized and made a choice not to mess with married men again."

Rhonda gave Tina an awkward look as if everything she had just said was not her problem. Tina also knew that look meant not to judge her until she judged herself. Rhonda was right.

Tina had already paid for all her wrongdoing to Rhonda and didn't want karma knocking on her door anymore. She didn't like her at all. Somehow, she kept coming around in the form of Rhonda. How many times could Tina apologize to her? She was sorry and was over everything that had happened in the past. She wanted Rhonda to be over it too.

Over time, Tina had been engaged a total of

four times to four different guys but never married. A part of it was that she looked in the mirror and found that she was wearing the pants and the skirt in the relationships. It wasn't because she wanted to; Lord knows she didn't! It was because she had to. She was forced to carry the load in every relationship and opted not to submit to them because of it. She was also afraid that if she'd ever gotten married, Rhonda would come after her husband with her bag of tricks.

As time went on, she realized that if a woman could steal her husband away, then he was never truly hers to begin with. Although she was done with karma, karma was not done with her. *What if my husband gets weak and falls into Rhonda's trap?* Tina would probably find herself on America's Most Wanted.

It was rumored (and Tina strongly believed) that Rhonda slept with John Brooke, Tina's ex, but they both denied it. She questioned him about the rumor, and everything that came out of his mouth seemed to draw a huge smile across his face and give him a little chuckle. Tina, of course, didn't see anything that he should be smiling about. Although he denied it, Tina had a vivid dream of John admitting to sleeping with Rhonda on five different occasions at his apartment. The way he smelled and dressed was exquisite, so she could see why Rhonda was drawn to him. His personality was amazing, and his charm was out of this world.

Rhonda wasn't done with Tina just yet. She and Tina's ex-boyfriend, Richard Johnson, worked at the same company. He was a lawyer, and she was his administrative specialist. She had a slim body and was looking sexy. He was debonair. She enticed him a lot by wearing low-cut shirts displaying her small, perky breasts. She would purposely bend over in front of him whenever she was at his desk so he could get a clear view of her mountain peaks. Because they were rather small, she never had to wear a bra. Her nipples showed through whatever shirt she wore, which was deemed inappropriate in the workplace.

She also wore short skirts that would show the bottom of her butt cheeks every time she had to bend over to pick something up off of the floor. When she sat down with her legs spread, it was evident that she wasn't wearing any panties. She knew exactly what she was doing and wanted him to see all that he could have with her. He ignored her come-and-get-it approaches, but she was unknowingly casting a spell on Richard. They both knew the magnitude of the relationship that he and Tina had had in the past, but how much longer could he resist the temptation?

When she realized she had his undivided attention, she began to act like a damsel in distress. She needed his help with everything, including walking to her car during lunch and after work. He started walking her to her car regularly, which caused them to talk more. They would sit in her car and talk for hours before they went their separate ways. Those talks turned into them exchanging little love taps.

Richard was getting to know Rhonda outside of being Tina's best friend, and he liked it. The only problem was Rhonda didn't care anything about him. She had no feelings for him whatsoever. She just wanted him between her legs so that she could say that she had had him without her best friend having a clue about it. She then began to pour on her flirtatious nature to seal the deal. At this moment, it took little effort because his nose was now wide open. She had him, and she knew it.

Rhonda gave him her cell number to contact her as soon as possible. He wasted no time calling her. They would talk about work, hobbies, dinner, and nighttime routines before they went to bed, alone. Then, they started having phone sex. She would tell him the things that she wanted to do to him, like turning his banana into a hot fudge sundae with all her favorite toppings, which would end with his homemade whipped cream and her tongue as a cherry on top for her to devour. These were things that Tina used to do to him, so he knew she must have discussed their lovemaking sessions with Rhonda. How else would she know? And, of course, what Tina didn't know couldn't hurt her.

All that sex talk got them both wanting to get together alone so that they could take care of business. They went out on dates to really get to know each other. Richard slowly started to catch feelings for Rhonda. Rhonda felt something, too, but she was sure it was just her lady parts throbbing for his touch. She was incapable of real feelings being that her heart had turned cold as ice. She only wanted to get her rocks off with him. Finally, they set a date and time to meet up at Rhonda's apartment to turn their fantasies into reality.

Richard arrived at Rhonda's apartment around nine o'clock one Saturday night looking better than he usually did in his grey and white Nike short set. She didn't hesitate to invite him inside and offer him something to drink. To her surprise, he had already stopped and picked up a bottle of her favorite wine. Although this made her smile, she was looking for a reason to flaunt her sexy tight-fitting mid-thigh-length red dress.

They were sitting on the couch listening to

music, talking about any and everything they could think of. Then came a moment of awkward silence. They were just staring at each other with scintillating looks in their eyes.

Rhonda asked Richard, "What's on your mind?" He didn't answer her but reached in, grabbed her face, pulled it to his, and kissed her in a way that he had never kissed Tina. He wanted to make sure she'd remember it, but she couldn't have cared less about that kiss. She was a jaded woman and wanted him inside of her as soon as possible.

Rhonda began to slide her dress down, further exposing her bare breasts. Then her dress fell to her hips. Richard could now see that not only was she not wearing a bra, she wasn't wearing panties either. Very excited, he rushed to slide his boxers and shorts down to his knees while still sitting on the couch and lifted her up with both hands.

They both began to rock, roll, whine, and jump to the beat of the old school rap music playing in the background as if they were dancing at a club. By the time the second song was over, so were they. Their heart rates had dropped back down to normal. Not only was the scent of their perfume and cologne everywhere, so was the scent of their natural body nectar.

Rhonda had gotten what she wanted, and that was to have something that she could throw in Tina's face. They both pulled their clothing back to its rightful place and continued to hang out on the couch. Around two o'clock in the morning, Richard finally got up and drove home.

Later that same day, on the phone, Richard and Rhonda made plans to hang out again the following Saturday at the same time and place. He told her that before they could hang out anymore, she needed to tell Tina what they were doing and had done. Rhonda couldn't understand why he wanted her to tell Tina. After all, they weren't together anymore, so for her, it wasn't a big deal. However, Richard had mad respect for Tina.

Rhonda believed it was guilt because if he'd really respected her, he wouldn't have given in to the temptation of sleeping with her best friend. Rhonda agreed to talk with Tina.

After hours of figuring out how she would approach the situation with Tina and what she would say, Rhonda called and told her that she and Richard had smashed each other. She had assured her that they were not in a relationship and that they were just friends with benefits. Tina was shocked that Richard would do this, but not at Rhonda's thirst. Tina just kind of laughed it off and pretended to be okay with it. She went as far as to invite them both over to her place for game night the next night. She wanted to see how they were around each other and if he was treating Rhonda like he treated her when they were in a serious relationship. Tina knew that even though Rhonda just wanted sex from Richard, he was probably really feeling Rhonda and wanted to commit to her. He was a one-woman man.

The next day, after much thought, Tina called Rhonda and asked, "How could you do that to me? Accept my sloppy seconds?" Tina then threatened to fight her on sight. Tina didn't mean it but was very hurt at Rhonda's antics. She honestly thought that they were done with all the messing around with each other's men. Rhonda laughed at Tina's idle threat and dared her to cross her path. Rhonda took it a step further and began to rub in Tina's face how good

Richard's microphone felt inside of her studio that night. That pissed Tina off to no end.

Richard realized what Rhonda was doing this whole time and how he had fallen right into her web. Her skills matriculated him into her well-designed plot to hurt Tina. The only problem was, he had caught feelings for her and wanted to title her as his lady. Unfortunately, Rhonda only wanted two things from Richard - what he could do for her financially and sexually. Eventually, he broke it off with Rhonda because she couldn't give him what he wanted, which was a committed relationship. He remembered that with Tina he had the whole package and then some.

Richard still tried to get Rhonda to feel toward him the way he felt toward her, but it just didn't work. Also, because Tina came around more often, and they all remained friends, it made everything awkward. What were they going to talk about? Because Tina and Rhonda were best friends, Richard removed himself from the equation completely and would only speak to them in passing. Rhonda, still carrying a grudge, had more to prove to Tina by way of revenge.

Back in the day, Rhonda had introduced Tina to Donnell Jenkins, and they became an official couple. Tina didn't think anything weird about it because once again, she forgave Rhonda for her past transgressions. Besides, she didn't have the temerity to ask Rhonda if this was a setup. She was just so happy that they were both in meaningful relationships at the same time and felt nothing could go wrong, as far as cheating with each other's men went. All was well for the time being. They would have couples' game nights together. They would even go out on double dates regularly. Everyone seemed elated, but there was something that Tina didn't know about

Rhonda and Donnell.

Tina had no clue that Donnell originally wanted to talk to Rhonda and that she had turned him down because she was in a relationship at the time. Otherwise, she would not have messed around with him at all. Rhonda had no intention of telling Tina, either, even though Rhonda had plenty of opportunities to say, "Donnell tried to holla at me first, girl, but I shot him down." If Tina had known that in the beginning, she wouldn't have given him the time of day. Instead, she was already in too deep. She thanked Rhonda on different occasions for introducing them to one another. Donnell was now Tina's beau thang. He got along well with her kids, and she felt that he was going to be a permanent fixture to her little family.

Rhonda broke up with her then-boyfriend because he was too controlling. She couldn't take his crazy, paranoid ways. He would sneak and look through her phone to see if she was talking to other guys. He put a tracker on her car to see if she was going where she actually said she was going. He was able to track her whereabouts by an app he had on his phone. Whenever he came home from work, he would make her take off her panties so that he could smell them and her vagina. He believed that he could tell if she had been sleeping around with someone else by doing this. He even began to tell her what she could and couldn't wear. He also tried to control who she could hang out with. Rhonda was truly done with this guy and back on the prowl, with a vindictive spirit, to interrupt Tina's life.

At this stage in their relationship, Tina and Donnell were having problems, especially with communicating. He took it upon himself, because they were best friends, to run to Rhonda to see what was up with Tina and the way she was acting. Of course, Rhonda welcomed him into her apartment with open arms. She intended to welcome him with open legs as well before all was said and done. Basically, Rhonda fed Donnell a bunch of bull that she knew would one day lead to his and Tina's breakup. She didn't care about helping them stay together at all, even though she was pretending to be his consoler.

Hours later, Rhonda pulled out a bottle of Patron and poured her and Donnell a drink, straight with no chaser. She ended up getting drunk and wanted him in her bed by any means necessary. So, she put on her rap music and turned the volume up as loud as they could stand. The song that was playing was "Pop That Coochie" by 2 Live Crew. She began to booty shake aggressively on Donnell while he was sitting on her couch. He's looking at her like, "Girl, you're wilding out." In his mind, he was like, "You know I'm with Tina, but still I admire all of your curves and dance skills." She continued dancing until he couldn't take it anymore. Roughness made him thrive and throb.

Rhonda had ignited a spark in Donnell that he just could not turn off even if he'd tried. The front of his tan jogging pants began to stand at attention. In Rhonda's mind, she was like bingo, I got him. Donnell, standing six feet and three inches, scooped Rhonda off her feet into his arms, sensually but assertively, and walked her to her bedroom. He then proceeded to lie her down on her queen-size bed and rip off every piece of clothing that she had on along with his white T-shirt. There was no time to gently take her clothes off. He was ready to bust it open with no remorse.

He quickly kicked his shoes off and stepped out of his pants. Because he was more into old school R&B, metaphorically, he first hit Rhonda with a "Downtown" by SWV. Then he did a "let me lick you up and down until you say stop" from Silk's song "Freak Me." Finally, with her legs spread open and positioned over his shoulders, he did a body blow and flatlined her with "give me some good love" by H-Town, "Knockin' da Boots." When they were all done and just lying there staring at the ceiling, he was playing in his mind, "As We Lay" by Shirley Murdock and Rhonda was playing in her head, "Nann" by Trick Daddy featuring Trina.

She told him that it was time for him to go because she was done with him and had other things to do. She was a straight savage, and all plaudits went to her. She blamed it all on the alcohol to justify what she had done with Donnell. She figured since he originally wanted her first, she didn't do anything wrong. They agreed to keep their mouths shut about what happened between them and to carry on as such.

The next morning, Rhonda remembered that they didn't use protection the night before and that she wasn't taking her birth control pills properly. Because of that, she needed to go to a drugstore to get the day after pill just to make sure there were no slip ups. She texted Donnell, letting him know what she'd done and how much money he needed to reimburse her for it. He was cool with it and wasn't sweating it. After all, he was still in a relationship with his girl, Tina.

Tina felt something was wrong with Donnell. She sensed that something was off, so she went through his phone while he was in the shower and found inappropriate pictures that he sent of himself to Rhonda. She couldn't fathom what she'd seen with her own eyes. There was no way that he could try to say that it wasn't him because Tina recognized the football-shaped birthmark that was centered right above his pubic hairline. She was furious and didn't know if she should cry, slap fire out of him, or just break up with him. She was determined not to let Rhonda win again. So, she decided not to say anything to Donnell until she talked to Rhonda.

Tina attempted to contact Rhonda several times and got no answer. So, in a fit of rage, she eventually blocked her on her cell phone and on all of her social media platforms for a period of time. She couldn't believe that this girl had stabbed her in the back again. She thought for a split second that she would stoop to her level and get her back but knew deep down inside that she couldn't. She'd remembered karma and wanted no part of it. With that being said, she backed off and gathered her thoughts.

Rhonda didn't respond to any of Tina's attempts to contact her at that time because she felt like this was her and Donnell's mess, and they needed to figure it out. What was she going to say to her anyway? She would have given her another tired empty, "I'm sorry." She was just sitting back, laughing at the whole thing because she knew what it was all about. She knew that Tina had searched through Donnell's phone and found the naked pictures that he had sent to her. She knew how Tina operated when she suspected something. In her mind, she was like, that's what you get for sleeping with Wendell all those years ago.

Because Tina couldn't reach Rhonda to rip her a new one, she finally decided to confront Donnell about what she saw on his phone. Of course, he hit her with, "It wasn't me, and you didn't see my face in any of those pictures." She quickly reminded him of his birthmark. All he could do was put his head down because he knew he was caught red-handed. He couldn't lie his way out of this. He got down on his knees and begged and pleaded with her not to leave him. He said that he was sorry and that he didn't know what came over him. He stated that he would never cheat on her again. Because she loved him and she knew that he loved her, she agreed to stay with him and give him another chance. Donnell waited on Tina hand and foot trying to make up for the pain he caused her on that lustful night he spent with Rhonda.

Tina and Donnell tried to hang in there and make their estranged relationship work, but there was no fixing it. Shortly after, their relationship ended all because of Rhonda. She couldn't trust those two anymore, especially around each other. She didn't want to deal with Donnell at all after that, but her and Rhonda's broken relationship stayed intact. Surely, this was the end of Rhonda's "I'm going to get you back" madness or was it?

Tina always bragged about how much her older boyfriend, Jesse Carter, would never cheat on her. She felt more comfortable saying that this time because he was well established. She figured he was done playing the field. Besides, she was beautiful, fine, and intelligent. Why would he want to cheat on her? He wasn't the greatest-looking guy in the world, but he was very charming. The day would soon come when someone would call her bluff and spill the tea on her oh-so-faithful boyfriend, who was, in fact, a cheater.

None other than Rhonda was there to oblige. She was able to see right through Jesse and knew he was an easy target. She knew this because he would always look at her like he was undressing her with his eyes. He was an old nasty-looking perverted man, and she couldn't wait to expose him to Tina indirectly.

One day after he'd dropped Tina off at home, he drove by the bus stop and saw Rhonda walking home. He stopped near her and asked, "Hey, do you need a ride home?"

"No, thanks!"

"Well, will you at least let me talk to you for a second?" In her mind, she thought, *I got him. I'll tell him all the nasty things that I want to do with him. He'll be so aroused. He'll take me to a nice hotel so that we can get it popping and chill for a minute.*

On the way to the hotel, Jesse made sure he checked in with Tina. He wanted to let her know that he was on his way home and would probably go to bed early. He did this so that she wouldn't call his phone until in the morning. This gave him the time he needed to do his dirt and get away with it.

Once they arrived at the Holiday Inn Express, checked in, and grabbed a bag of items from his trunk, they walked to the room. She remembered when walking through the hotel door, he had the song "Superwoman" by Karen White playing on his phone. She went straight to the bathroom to freshen up. When she came back out, she saw that Jesse had wasted no time getting undressed and sprawling out on the queen-size bed. His unmentionables were just flopping in the wind.

He reached over on the nightstand and grabbed his bag of goodies that he had gotten from the car. To Rhonda's surprise, he was low key into that bondage crap. He pulled a blindfold, some handcuffs, some oil, a large leather thong, and a whip out of the bag and placed them on the bed. Most of those items were for him. Being that she was down for whatever, she followed suit.

Rhonda stripped down to her bare essentials as well. After he got up off the bed and put on the thong, he got back on the bed in a doggy position. He instructed her to spank him on his butt really hard for being such a bad boy. She couldn't help but laugh because she was silly like that, but she did exactly what she was told. After spanking him at least ten times, he was so turned on and ready to have Rhonda.

With both of them standing on their feet at the end of the bed, he told her to turn around (with her back facing him) so that he could put the blindfold on her, which she did. He then told her to bend over and place her arms behind her back as if she was being arrested. After handcuffing her and taking the thong off, he used the oil as a lubricant for his rather large elephant trunk and then mated with Rhonda like he was in a wild African jungle. He bucked and thrust so much and so hard that before he knew it, his Safari ride was over. The loud, roaring sound he was making and the shaking that he was doing was sure proof of that. That was a real Coming to America experience. She enjoyed herself too because this all was different and new to her. As soon as he uncuffed her, they got dressed and continued with small talk until they decided to leave.

Rhonda had Jesse drop her off at her cousin's house so she would have an alibi if Tina got suspicious and started asking questions. She didn't want to tell Tina herself. Otherwise, she would have just called Tina to meet her at the hotel and busted him in that manner. Rhonda began to think that he was a fraud because while he was in the hotel checking in, she snooped through the glove compartment and saw that Tina's name was on the car he was so proudly driving.

The next day Rhonda made sure to spark a conversation with the gossip group. She kept saying, "Tina thinks she's got a good man, but she doesn't." She repeated it continuously because she knew eventually one of them would ask her, "Why do you say that?" That was her cue to tell them all that happened the night before with her and Jesse at the hotel. She knew that one of them, if not all, would run back and tell Tina all that was said. Rhonda honestly didn't care because she felt nothing. She did it because she was hurting inside.

The word on the street was that Tina had heard all the gossip of Jesse supposedly sleeping with Rhonda. She got all the juicy details about everything that transpired at the Holiday Inn Express with her man and best friend. Tina was exhausted from trying to continue loving her best friend and continuously forgiving her.

She didn't really confront Rhonda this time, but she did let her know that she had broken up with Jesse for good because she found out that he had cheated on her with some trifling hoe. The look on Rhonda's face told it all. Tina really questioned their friendship at that point. She took a break from hanging out with her for a long while to regroup mentally and emotionally. For the life of her, she just could not end their friendship.

Rhonda and Tina's friendship were back on good terms after they talked things out. Rhonda knew that Tina and Enrique Samson were in a relationship, but she pretended to hate his guts and only tolerated him because of Tina. She would say things like, "He's not the one for you" and "He's no good." All the while, she knew that she wanted to sink her fangs into him, figuratively speaking. He was a Trevante Rhodes look-alike, and she wanted a piece of him. She was going to play this game until she got him and that piece. Trust, she had already scoped out the size and length of his stake from the print she saw through his jeans. That was just when it was at ease, so she really was curious about what he was working with down there. She planned to soon find out.

Rhonda was invited over to Tina and Enrique's place several times for dinner, and she always showed up. She would never turn down a home-cooked meal. While eating dinner one evening, Tina told Rhonda and her boyfriend that she would be going out of town for the weekend, job-related. She told Rhonda that she could still come over and wash her clothes if she wanted to. Everything on Rhonda's body perked up to this splendid news. Tina didn't think twice about it because she knew that Rhonda really couldn't stand the ground that Enrique walked upon, and Tina trusted him.

Saturday afternoon came, and Rhonda headed over to Tina and Enrique's place to wash two loads of clothes. He let her in with no problem and continued to watch the football game in the living room. She didn't even speak. She just walked into the laundry room and started her laundry. When she went into the laundry room, she was fully dressed. When she came out, she only had on a shirt and panties. Enrique told her to put on some clothes. She began to argue back and forth with him, which in actuality, was arousing her. Rhonda then slapped him across the face, which caused him to grab her hands so that she couldn't do it again. She pretended to pull away, and he pulled her to him, face to face, and said aggressively, "Don't hit me again!" She quickly turned her head sideways and kissed him. He stepped back in utter shock, still holding on to her hands. She leaned in to kiss him again, and he just stared at her in disbelief. She did it again, and this time he didn't pull away. In fact, he kissed her back, letting go of her hands, and pulled her into his arms, close to his body.

Enrique was wearing jeans with no shirt or socks. He ushered Rhonda over to the loveseat and told her to get into the doggy position on the chair. Being the vampire that she was, she pulled her panties to the side, allowing him with unzipped jeans to stab his stake into the heart of her warm place. They both began to bleed pulsating passion over and over again until he hit the final nail in her coffin. Some would call it a quickie, but they called it Transylvania. Now that they were done and dead, Tina would surely kill them if she ever found out.

They went on with life like nothing ever happened. Rhonda finished washing, drying, and folding her clothes without saying anything else to Enrique. He continued watching the football game, trying to figure out if he should tell Tina. Eventually, Rhonda went home. They both were nasty and disgusting to have had sex with each other, period, let alone in that girl's house while she was away on business. They knew that Tina was returning home the next day. They couldn't control their hormones for one more day or go somewhere else?!? That was a low blow, even for Rhonda.

Tina arrived home on that Sunday evening and noticed that Enrique did not greet her like he usually would. She thought it was odd but didn't question him. She figured that he was just preoccupied with something. She carried on with her normal everyday activities but realized that he hadn't tried to have sex with her yet. He had a really high sex drive, so she knew something was up. She walked over to him, looking directly into his eyes and asked him, "What is wrong with you?" He confessed what happened between him and Rhonda the day before. Tina, very calmly, told Enrique that their relationship was over. She instructed him to pack all of his belongings and leave now. He knew that because she was so mild-mannered, he should quickly pack and get out of Dodge. He knew that this was the calm before the storm and that she was giving him a chance to continue living. Tina was more concerned about seeing and talking to Rhonda. That's who she really was angry with for the eleventeenth time.

Tina finally ran into Rhonda at the gas station near her apartment. Rhonda had been ignoring her since she'd been back home. She was avoiding Tina because Enrique had already given her the heads up that he told her what took place between them that Saturday afternoon.

"How was your weekend? Did you get all of your clothes washed?"

"Yes, I did!" She rolled her eyes at her and apologized for sleeping with her man as if she was doing Tina a favor by admitting to what she already knew. At this time, Rhonda was beginning to sound like a broken record. Tina wondered if her best friend was ever going to stop torturing her. Would she ever show any signs of having a contrite heart? Tina would someday find out that the answer to her question might be what finally ended their so-called friendship.

Tina had gotten engaged to a handsome young man named Desmond Pride. They were very much in love and ready to spend the rest of their lives together.

One day while she and Rhonda were hanging out having girl talk, she noticed that Rhonda was not happy about her engagement. Rhonda couldn't stand the fact that Tina was getting married and she wasn't. She tried to be happy for her, but she just couldn't. She couldn't figure out how this was happening. Tina was the one who started this whole betrayal thing, but she would be the one to finish it. Rhonda was very adamant about not letting her have a happy ending.

Tina knew that Rhonda was adjusting to her and Desmond being engaged. She thought it would be good to have Desmond and Rhonda help with some of the wedding planning if she wasn't available. What was Tina thinking?? Did she not have a modicum of sense? A blind man could see that Rhonda had not changed. Rhonda's eyes lit up from this good news. She knew it was time to plan for Operation Finish Him, and she was ready for war.

A few weeks later, Desmond saw Rhonda as he drove by her house and waved at her. Of course, she waved back with much-anticipated flirting. He wasn't really sure how to take that, so an hour later he called her.

"Were you flirting with me earlier?

"Of course!"

"Why?"

"Because I think you're very handsome."

He was intrigued by what he'd heard. He felt that there was nothing wrong with a little harmless teasing. He knew his boundaries and would never cross that line. They were only supposed to be helping with planning the wedding, not making romantic gestures at each other.

That same day they decided to meet up and talk in person. Rhonda made her way over to Tina's place. Tina was at work, and Desmond had the day off. He was in the laundry room when Rhonda walked in. He looked at her like a soldier who desperately wanted to enter her battlefield. They grabbed each other and kissed so deeply as if grenades were going off around them. They both quickly undressed in an attempt to camouflage themselves away from the enemy.

He picked her up off the floor and placed her on the washing machine. Then he gently tilted her back at a slight angle, so that her foxhole would meet his weapon of mass destruction. Desmond took his M16, positioned himself correctly into her foxhole, and fired several rounds with the help of the washing machine's vibration. He was aiming for the kill. After all, he had medals for being a sharpshooter in the military.

Rhonda and Desmond could have picked a more comfortable area of the apartment, like the couch or the bedroom, to go to war, but most of it was filthy, as Tina hadn't cleaned up that day. Once the battle was won, they got dressed and carried on with the wedding planning like nothing had ever happened between them. This was their little secret that they wanted to keep.

Rhonda went home, and she and Desmond continued meeting several times after that to have sex. She believed that he really loved her and was eventually going to leave Tina. This one particular day, he noticed that she was a little too clingy toward him.

"You're not getting attached, are you?"

"No, silly."

He boldly let her know that he would never leave Tina, how much he was in love with her, and couldn't wait to marry her. Rhonda couldn't believe what she was hearing. Her blood began to boil with anger. She still managed to smile and laugh through her pain.

Through her rage, Rhonda realized that Desmond was just using her and had no intention of leaving Tina for her. She knew she had to get back at them both somehow. Surely, Desmond had to know that he had barked up the wrong tree toying with her feelings. He had to know that she was going to tell Tina everything that had happened with them behind her back and how often. Desmond really didn't think everything through. He honestly believed that Rhonda would never breathe a word to anyone, let alone Tina.

Rhonda couldn't wait for Tina to get off from work that day so that she could tell her the secret that she'd been keeping. In fact, she drove to Tina's job and sat in the parking lot until she walked out of the building to her car. Rhonda was so bent on spilling all the tea that she did not once care about the consequences. Perhaps, she thought that Tina was going to forgive her again like she had always done in the past. She really didn't care; she just didn't want them to get married.

Upon seeing Rhonda sitting in the car outside of her job, Tina already knew something was wrong because this had never happened before. She approached Rhonda's car and could see she was in tears. She signaled for her to let down the window.

"What's wrong?"

Rhonda, barely able to get her words out, revealed to Tina, "I slept with Desmond more than once, and I've fallen for him." She also told her that he still wanted to marry her. Tina walked away in silence. She really couldn't put all the blame on

Rhonda. She could no longer stomach looking at her. That girl had crossed the point of no return, and Tina was done with giving her passes. She left her right there in the parking lot and drove home. Their friendship was indeed over. Now it was time for Tina to come face to face with Desmond.

Did he really sleep with Rhonda, or was she making this up? Should she work things out with him and still marry him? Her mind raced with thoughts as she drove home. She kept hearing Rhonda say that they'd slept together more than once. It didn't take her long to quickly come to her senses.

When she pulled up in her driveway, he was standing outside on the front porch. Tina stormed out of the car directly toward him and started windmilling the heck out of him. She called him every unpleasant name that she could think of. She took off the engagement ring and threw it at him. The wedding was off. She told him to go marry Rhonda since he was screwing her.

At this stage, he figured out that Rhonda had opened her big mouth. He definitely didn't want Rhonda, but he knew he had blown the best relationship he'd ever had. He gracefully gathered all of his belongings, including his face and heart off the ground, left and didn't look back. He'd caused too much damage between Tina and Rhonda. After crying for months and going through bouts of depression, Tina moved on—without Desmond or Rhonda, of course.

In the end, Rhonda got what she wanted, and that was to break off their engagement. She felt that she had won, but she really didn't. It's safe to say that Rhonda would eventually get her proper dose of karma. One thing about karma, she always wins.

It appeared that she had to try out whoever Tina loved. Not the guys that she just liked but loved. Rhonda was damaged and hurt. As the saying goes, "Hurt people hurt people!" However, a damaged and broken individual recognizes another damaged and broken individual. This was why Tina was so adamant about holding onto their friendship, no matter the cost. Underneath all that hurt and pain, she knew Rhonda had a kind heart and spirit. She understood why she chose the route of self-medicating. Tina could see through her pain because she knew what it looked like and what it felt like. She figured that if she'd healed, then Rhonda could eventually heal through prayer and counseling, too. Tina realized over time that enough was enough, and that karma was indeed no joke!

Karma

There is a girl that goes and comes back around,
And Karma is her name-a.
K-A-R-M-A
K-A-R-M-A
K-A-R-M-A
And Karma is her name-a.

If you open the door to her,
She will come in.

She doesn't care about you,
She just releases her wrath.

The grief and pain that you caused,
You will feel and reflect.

She couldn't care less about what you look, act, or sound
like,
Remember, you came for her.

Karma comes for hers,
And won't stop until she collects.

Chapter 7
The Ultimate Revenge

Thirty-four years later, Tina decided to reach out to Wendell to get some important information from him that she needed for one of her short films. She wanted information about his life in the United States Marine Corps and the places he had traveled while on active duty. She began to realize that she had a gift for writing short films. That was truly the only reason she called him at first, nothing more or nothing less. She assumed that he was still married, and she was never going to mess around with a married man again, knowingly or unknowingly.

She first sent him a personal message on Facebook Messenger to let him know why she was trying to contact him, but she never received a response. On Facebook Messenger, it can be seen when a person has read a message, and he never read the message that she sent. Tina then Googled him and came across his phone number and address. She called one of the numbers and got no answer. She left a voice message but got no callback.

The next day she texted the number asking, "Does this number belong to a Wendell Raynor?" The person texted back, saying, "No, it does not." She then called the employer listed on his Facebook page. The lady who answered could not locate his name in the workplace directory. The lady transferred Tina to their

HR Department to see if Wendell still worked there. After holding for a while, she just hung up the phone.

She then dialed another number that she had found on Google. To her surprise and mere serendipity, she heard a while-you-wait ringtone of a Marine Corps cadence and knew it had to be the correct number for Wendell. She left a voice message for him explaining why she had reached out to him.

He eventually called her back, but Tina couldn't answer her phone, so he left her a voice message. After she heard his deep sexy voice on her voice mail saying, "Hello, Tina! How you doing? You know who this is," her entire body from head to toe reacted. Even the fine hairs on her body stood up, and she wasn't sure why. Was it because she'd been celibate for many years now? How could he have this kind of effect on her after all this time? He had awakened feelings in her, some that she'd never felt before and others that she hadn't felt in a long time. She wasn't expecting these feelings because she had no intention of dating outside of her race again. She listened to his voicemail at least ten more times. They then played phone tag before they finally got to talk to each other.

When they did talk to each other, it was like magic, at least to Tina. She asked him the questions that she needed for her project, and she was pretty much done with the conversation. She was nervous and really didn't have much more to say or know what else to say. Wendell began to ask her how was she doing, and what had she been up to? She answered his questions. He began to tell her very intimate details about his life.

He told her about what he liked, what he could bring to the table, his love for God, his family, his deep-rooted issues, that he was single, and that he was a very busy man. She did the same and let him know that she was single too. He was also interviewing Tina as if she could possibly be his future mate, or so she thought. He seemed to be very interested in her. She was interviewing him as well.

She found him fascinating and discovered through their conversation that they had a lot in common. They shared the same Christian beliefs, they both were homebodies, and they both lost their moms to heart/lung issues. They even shared the fact that they had scars on their faces. He had a scar, from a job accident, near his jawline, and she had a scar, from a childhood accident, on her face near her temple.

He really spilled his heart out to her, which she thought was very odd for a man right off the bat. She wanted to get to know Wendell, the man who had developed from the boy she knew back in high school. Tina was sure that God had finally sent the man that He had chosen just for her. She thought that because they didn't get closure in the past, this was their chance to start a new relationship as adults, especially after learning that he only lived an hour away from her in the next county and that he passed by her subdivision every day on his way to and from work. She thought that she would have a new friend to hang out with and talk to if nothing else.

Tina had to cut the conversation short because she had to attend a gala with one of her sons. So, she ended by saying that she had to go and that she wasn't looking for a relationship, but she was open to trying one if that's what their future communication led to. That was what she meant anyway. He said that maybe they could meet up somewhere, have a beverage, and catch up. She was down for that and assumed that it would happen soon since they had not seen each other in many years. Tina was so anxious to see what he looked like now. She wanted to give him the biggest hug in the whole wide world. She wanted to see his reaction to seeing her again. She was anxious to see if there was some type of spiritual connection there, and she wanted to hear his deep voice in person. Tina was smiling from ear to ear for the rest of the day and night.

Over the next couple of days, she shared with her kids and best friend that she had contacted an old friend whom she messed around with back in high school. She told them how great their communication was and that they were supposed to meet up soon to hang out. She pulled up his Facebook pictures to show them, and they said that he was a good-looking guy. Her daughter said that he was cute and had smooth-looking skin. Of course, Tina thought that he was still handsome and fine. His grey hair made him look very distinguished, which was the type of man she'd liked. The pictures were not current, though.

After two weeks had passed, she still hadn't heard from Wendell. Surely, she should have seen him by now. Didn't he want to see her and get to know the woman that she was today? She couldn't believe that he hadn't contacted her by now. She decided to text his number to let him know that she was very interested in getting to know him. She got no response. She included in that text her home address, hoping that he would just stop by her house at any time. Well, at a respectable time. Apparently, he didn't catch on because he never stopped by.

The Thanksgiving holiday was coming up. She texted him again the day before, inviting him over for Thanksgiving dinner with her and her family if he didn't already have plans. A couple of hours later, he responded by saying that he already had plans with his family but thanked her for the invite. Tina was just ecstatic that he responded to her text. She thought, *how is it that he responded to my second text, but not to my previous messages? Is he ignoring me? Clearly, he got my first text, as well. What was the deal with this man?*

Two more weeks passed by and again, no word from Wendell. At this time, Tina was like, "Forget him!" She knew she was a good woman, a virtuous woman. It would be his loss. On the other hand, she thought she should just send him a good morning text with a current picture of her, which she did. Still, no response. She was really done with trying to let him know that she was interested and wanted to get to know him. His vagaries could no longer be overlooked.

However, she did wonder if he already had a girlfriend. Was he not attracted to her? Was she not skinny enough? Was it because she rocked her natural hair? Were they not friends? Was he not interested in her? Although she knew he was a busy man, she also knew that if he was really interested in her, he would have sacrificed time for her. One thing Tina wasn't going to do was run behind a man. She wondered if he was no longer into African-American women or if she said something wrong that turned him off? She'd surely hoped not because she planned to live well into her nineties, just like her great grandmother did. Her blood pressure and diuretic medications would make sure of that.

She could still do most of the things that she'd previously done, but with certain things (climbing stairs, long walks, etc.), she had to stop and take breaks. Did he view her no longer working, due to her heart disability, as a sign of weakness? Did he think she wanted material things from him? Tina had her own and wanted nothing from him but him. Material things didn't impress her, but a man's actions and his time did. Could he learn to love someone like her? She was ready to open her heart to him and let him in. She was ready to love him unconditionally. She was ready to shower him with affection. She was ready to trust and submit to her king. She was ready to love again! Tina never reached out to him again and would never have her questions answered. She was a little disappointed that he didn't allow her to get to know him and that he didn't get to know her. She was appalled that he didn't get to see how she had matured and how God had changed her inside out. She also felt rejected but quickly remembered her self-worth and that she was more than enough. She honestly believed that they could've had true love together, but then she had to snap back into reality. She began to think that just maybe she dodged a bullet. Perhaps, Wendell not wanting Tina in the way that she'd foreseen was the ultimate payback for what she had done to Rhonda and Webster.

"Be anxious for nothing, but in everything by prayer and supplication, with thanksgiving, let your requests be made known to God; and the peace of God, which surpasses all understanding, will guard your hearts and minds through Christ Jesus" (New King James Version, Php. 4.6-8).

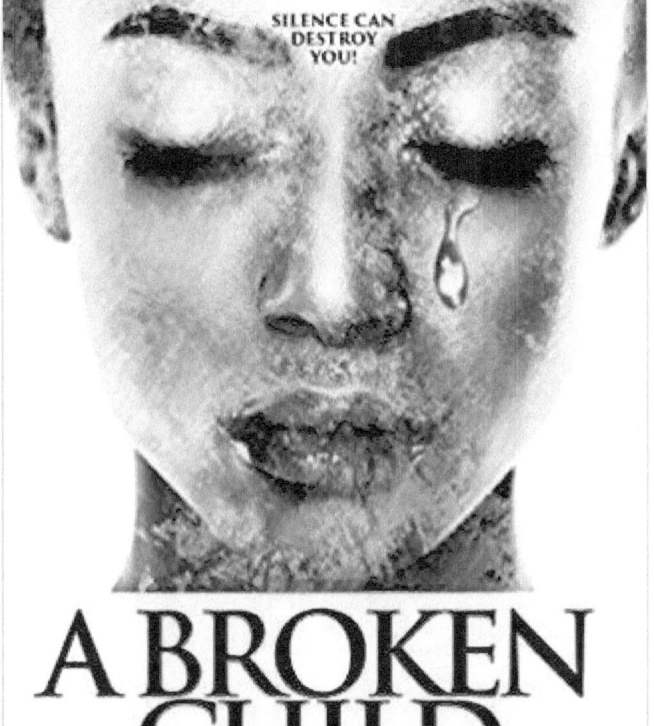

SILENCE CAN
DESTROY
YOU!

A BROKEN
CHILD

SAVED BY GOD'S GRACE

SHEILA DORSEY